Henry and Mudge
AND THE
Best Day of All

The Fourteenth Book of Their Adventures

Story by Cynthia Rylant
Pictures by Suçie Stevenson

Ready-to-Read
Aladdin Paperbacks

To Barbara Lalicki, for all her cheerleading—CR

For my nephews, Peter and Matthew Stevenson—SS

THE HENRY AND MUDGE BOOKS

First Aladdin Paperbacks Edition, 1997

Text copyright © 1995 by Cynthia Rylant
Illustrations copyright © 1995 by Suçie Stevenson

Aladdin Paperbacks
An imprint of Simon & Schuster Children's Publishing Division
1230 Avenue of the Americas
New York, NY 10020

The text of this book was set in 18 pt. Old Goudy.
The illustrations were rendered in pen-and-ink and watercolor.

Printed and bound in the United States of America.

30 29 28 27 26 25 24 23 22

The Library of Congress has catalogued the Simon & Schuster Books
for Young Readers Edition as follows:
Rylant, Cynthia.
Henry and Mudge and the best day of all / by Cynthia Rylant: illustrated by Suçie Stevenson.
p.   cm.
Summary: Henry and his big dog Mudge celebrate Henry's birthday with a piñata, a lively
birthday party, and a cake shaped like a fish tank, making May first the best day ever.
[1.Birthdays—Fiction. 2.Dogs—Fiction.] I.Stevenson, Suçie, ill. II.Title
PZ7.R982Heaj   1995
[E]-dc20   93-35939
ISBN 978-0-689-81006-0 (hc)
ISBN 978-0-689-81385-6 (pbk)

Contents

The First Day of May

On the first day of May
Henry woke up early
and said to his big dog Mudge,
"I'm having a birthday today."
Mudge wagged his tail, rolled over,
and snored.

"Mudge," said Henry, "wake up.
I'm having a birthday today."
Mudge wagged, rolled to the
other side, and snored some more.

"Mudge," said Henry, "*birthday cake*."

Mudge opened one eye.

"*Ice cream*," said Henry.

Mudge opened the other eye.

"And lots and lots of *crackers*,"
said Henry.

Mudge jumped up.

He shook Henry's hand.

Henry was having a birthday
and Mudge would be having crackers.
The first day of May
looked pretty good.

A Colorful Morning

Balloons were all over Henry's house.

Pink ones, orange ones, green ones,

yellow ones.

They were in the bathroom.

They were in the kitchen.

They were in the living room.

And the porch was full of them.

"Dad likes balloons,"
Henry told Mudge.
Mudge licked a yellow one
and wagged.

12

Henry's father came into the house.

He was carrying a camera.

"Pictures!" cried Henry's father.

"Oh no," Henry whispered to Mudge.

"Dad likes pictures, too."

Henry's father took lots of pictures.

He took one of Henry.

He took one of Mudge.

He took one of Henry and Mudge.

He took one of Henry and Mudge and
Henry's mother.
Then the bookcase took one
of all four of them.

After the pictures,
Henry's mother fixed Henry's
favorite breakfast,
pancakes with strawberries.
The family ate and ate and ate.

When they were done,
they had four very sticky
red mouths.

The first day of May
was looking even better.

Crackers from the Sky

Henry had invited his friends
for a party.
They came at three o'clock.
At first everyone was shy.
No one knew what to do.
Then Henry's mother said,
"Everybody outside!"

In the backyard
Henry's mother and Henry's father
had fixed games.
There was ringtoss.

There was go-fishing.

There were potato-sack races.

21

And hanging from a tree
was a big blue piñata
shaped like a donkey.

The winners at ringtoss
got decoder rings.
The winners at go-fishing
got baby goldfish.
The winners at potato-sack races
got bags of potato chips.

Finally it was time
for the piñata.
Henry's father tied a cloth
over Henry's eyes.
He put a stick in Henry's hand.
He whispered a message
in Henry's ear.
Then Henry started to swing.

"ONE!" everyone shouted.

"TWO!"

"THREE!"

Mudge was wagging hard.

"FOUR!"

On the fourth swing
the piñata cracked open.

Out fell suckers
and bubble gum
and taffy
and hundreds of little crackers.

Everyone was happy,
and Mudge most of all.
He never knew that
crackers could come from the sky.

Best Day

After the games
Henry's parents brought out
a big bowl of cherry-nut ice cream
and a very wide birthday cake.

The cake looked like
Henry's fish tank.
It had blue water,
colored rocks,
and striped and spotted fish.
Mudge sniffed and sniffed.
Maybe it looked like water,
but it smelled like *cake*.

After the fish-tank cake

was eaten up,

it was time to open presents.

Red bows, purple paper, big cards—

everything went flying in the air.

Henry got an airplane model,

a robot,

a stuffed snow leopard,

and a basketball.

He also got a box of
dog treats.
"These must be for you,"
Henry told Mudge.

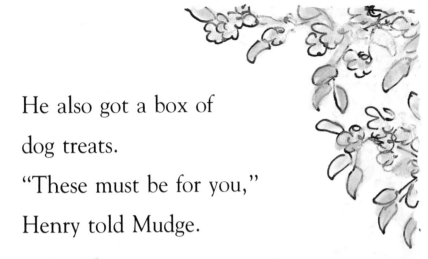

When the party was over,
everyone went home.
They all had lots of taffy and
bubble gum and suckers
and baby fish and potato chips.

They were full of cake and ice cream.

Some of them were full of crackers.

Henry and Henry's parents
and Henry's big dog Mudge
sat quietly in the backyard
and closed their eyes.
They listened to the birds.
They rested.

And each dreamed about birthday wishes
on the best day of all.

40